For Tara and Alexandra   KH
To Mary Craig with love   HC

Published by Pleasant Company Publications
© 2000 HIT Entertainment PLC
Text copyright © 1984 by Katharine Holabird
Illustrations copyright © 1984 by Helen Craig

Visit our Web site at www.americangirl.com

Printed in Italy.
00 01 02 03 04 05 06 LEGO 10 9 8 7 6 5 4 3 2 1

Library of Congress Cataloging-in-Publication Data
Craig, Helen.
Angelina and the Princess / illustrations by Helen Craig ;
story by Katharine Holabird.
p. cm.
Summary: Angelina is too sick to dance well during the tryouts for
the lead in the "Princess of Mouseland" ballet, but when the
leading ballerina sprains her foot, Angelina is ready to
prove she is still the best dancer of all.
ISBN 1-58485-148-1
[1. Mice—Fiction. 2. Ballet dancing—Fiction. 3. Dancers—Fiction.]
I. Holabird, Katharine. II. Title.
PZ7.C84418 Am 2000
[E]—dc21   00-022879

Angelina
and the Princess

Story by **Katharine Holabird** Illustrations by **Helen Craig**

PLEASANT COMPANY PUBLICATIONS™

Angelina was much too excited to sleep. The students at Miss Lilly's Ballet School had been asked to dance for Her Royal Highness, The Princess of Mouseland. Mr. Lightfoot, Director of the famous Royal Ballet Company, was coming tomorrow to help Miss Lilly choose the best ballerinas for the special performance. Angelina wanted a leading part so much that she worked on her pliés and pirouettes far into the night when she should have been sound asleep.

The next morning Angelina woke up feeling terrible.
Her head ached and her ears buzzed. Angelina's mother
took her temperature and shook her head sadly. "I'm
afraid you'll have to stay in bed," she said. "You can't
go to ballet school when you're not well."

But Angelina was determined to go. While her mother was busy downstairs, Angelina packed her ballet bag…

...and tiptoed out of the house.

Angelina arrived at Miss Lilly's Ballet School just in time to join her friends Flora and Felicity and all the other ballerinas who were waiting to go on stage. Flora did a nimble leap and a delicate spin…

…and then it was Angelina's turn to dance. Her heart started beating like a drum and she couldn't remember what she was supposed to be doing.

The music started and
Angelina knew she had
to begin. She tried one
step, she tried another…

…then she began twirling and spinning like a top until she was so dizzy she lost her balance, tripped on her pink ribbons, and tumbled down with a thump.

Flora and Felicity were given the leading roles in the
Dance of the Flower Fairies. Later, Miss Lilly called for
Angelina. "I'm afraid you will have to take a smaller
part this time," she said, trying to be kind.

When Angelina got home, her mother was very upset.
"How could you run away like that when I told you to
stay in bed?" she asked.

Angelina burst into tears. "I had to go to Miss Lilly's, but everything went wrong. I danced so badly for Mr. Lightfoot, I will never be a real ballerina. I am not going to ballet school any more."

Angelina's mother hugged her and kissed her and
carried her upstairs, and in just a minute she was
fast asleep in her own bed again.

The next day Angelina's headache was gone. She
felt better, but she was still very sad. "It's not fair!"
said Angelina.

"Maybe not," her mother said gently, "but things don't always go our way. You can still do your best with whatever part you are given, and that will help the whole performance."

Angelina thought about what her mother had said. Then she returned to Miss Lilly's after all, and rehearsed very hard with the other ballerinas for the Royal Performance.

After she had learned her own part, she memorized
the Dance of the Flower Fairies while watching
Flora and Felicity.

On the day of the Royal Performance, just as the show
was about to begin, Flora tripped and sprained her ankle.
Everyone was terribly upset.

Mr. Lightfoot and Miss Lilly turned to each other in horror. "Who can do the part?" they cried. Angelina was worried about Flora, but Susie stepped forward and said, "Angelina can!"

Angelina showed Miss Lilly that she had learned the dance by heart. "But what about Flora?" she asked. "Don't worry," said Miss Lilly, "we have a treat for her…"

…So Flora was happy because she was invited to sit right next to The Princess of Mouseland. Mr. Lightfoot and Miss Lilly were happy because the performance could go on. Angelina was happy because she did the Dance of the Flower Fairies without forgetting a single step. The Princess of Mouseland was happy because she loved ballet.

When the performance was over she congratulated Angelina
and thanked her warmly for saving the show.

A free catalogue for your little ballerina!

If you've fallen in love with Angelina Ballerina,™ you'll love the Little American Girl catalogue. Angelina's world comes to life in a line of charming playthings and girl-sized clothes that

complement her beautiful books. You'll also discover Bitty Baby,® a precious baby doll who has her own adorable line of clothes and accessories.

To receive your free catalogue, return this card, visit our Web site at **americangirl.com**, or call **1-800-845-0005**.

Send me a catalogue:

Name
_____

Address
_____

City   State   Zip
                                 86945i

My child's birth date: _____ / _____ / _____
                       month   day   year

Send my friend a catalogue:

Name
_____

Address
_____

City   State   Zip
                                 86947i

BUSINESS REPLY MAIL
FIRST-CLASS MAIL   PERMIT NO. 1137   MIDDLETON WI

POSTAGE WILL BE PAID BY ADDRESSEE

NO POSTAGE
NECESSARY
IF MAILED
IN THE
UNITED STATES

PO BOX 620497
MIDDLETON WI 53562-9940